A Coming of Winter
in the ADIRONDACKS

written by Brian J. Heinz

illustrated by Maggie Henry

North Country Books, Inc.

Utica, New York

ISBN-10 1-59531-038-X
ISBN-13 978-1-59531-038-5

Design by Zach Steffen & Rob Igoe, Jr.

Library of Congress Cataloging-in-Publication Data

Heinz, Brian J., 1946-
  A coming of winter in the Adirondacks / by Brian J. Heinz ; illustrated by Maggie Henry.
      p. cm.
  Summary: Birds and animals experience the snowy winter season in the Adirondack Mountains, as otters slide down a
riverbank into icy waters, red foxes romp in the white landscape, and bluejays chatter as if to announce the arrival of winter.
  ISBN 978-1-59531-038-5 (alk. paper)
  [1. Winter--Fiction. 2. Snow--Fiction. 3. Nature--Fiction. 4. Animals--Fiction. 5. Adirondack Mountains (N.Y.)--Fiction.] I. Healy,
Maggie, ill. II. Title.
  PZ7.H36855Co 2011
  [E]--dc22

                              2010040702

North Country Books, Inc.
220 Lafayette Street
Utica, New York 13502
www.northcountrybooks.com

For Mom, Lutz, Marie,
and our Adirondack neighbors
in Whiteface Meadows

— Brian J. Heinz

To all my teachers

— Maggie Henry

Winter is on its way and the High Peaks are in celebration. Hillsides and valleys look to be on fire as trees shimmer in the glow of autumn light. Green spires of hemlock and spruce poke their slender necks skyward as if to get a better view. For surely, Winter is coming.

There is a snap to the air, a dull
chill that snuck in as quiet as a breath. A
smattering of clouds crawls over the northern horizon.
The wind picks up and hisses through swaying treetops.
Branches quiver and leaves flutter like countless flags.

An endless parade of clouds marches across the sky,
climbing into a churning wall of gray. A vast
shadow races over the ground as the sun
is reduced to a sliver, then blotted out.

Now the animals know.
Winter is closing in.

In the abandoned orchard, white-tailed deer
feast on the last of fallen apples. The skins are
rusty and soft, the flesh as sweet and mushy as
applesauce. The buck and doe each raise their heads. Then,
with tails thrown high, they bound for the low ground, to
the sheltering thickets where they may lie in wait.

Beaver squats atop his lodge, clamping a chewed stick between his teeth. A cold breeze lifts the nap of his fur. His head snaps right, then left. Beaver plunges into the pond. Smack! His tail slaps the warning. *Hurry! Winter is almost here.*

Beaver dips below the surface. A moment later he shakes off the wetness, safe inside his lodge.

Even Black Bear is lumbering to her secret hideaway under a moss-draped log. She claws past a tangle of limbs, hunkers down in a bed of pine needles, and closes her eyes. She will sleep, for there is nothing to do but wait.

The wind rises in the forest like
the sound of rushing water,
then fades again to a whisper.

Chickadees make a mad flight for cover, weaving among trees in the darkening woods to a cluster of hemlocks. They snuggle in the bowered branches and puff themselves up like feathered balls.

Brook trout dart from under
the roiling shallows of the Ausable River to
deep and quiet pools tucked under stony ledges.

Then, at that magic moment... no longer day but not quite night... that fleeting instant between dark and light... the first flakes fall. Old Man Winter is here.

One massive cloud curls over the Keene Valley like a clenched fist. The grim sky drops onto the mountains. The rocky summits of Armstrong, Saddleback, and Gothics rake at the belly of the cloud, releasing whirling flurries. The wind swells to a howling rage and the sky unfolds in a furious shaking-out of snow.

Bobcat stirs in his den. It is an uneasy sleep
as the fierce music of the storm plays into the
darkness. There is the snapping of twigs. There is the
rattle of flying leaves. There is the groan of a great tree and
the sickening crack as it surrenders to the wind and the weight of
the snow. And there is that hour-after-hour whistle of arctic air.

But dawn arrives to silence and stillness.
The sun seems to rise a bit more slowly to illuminate
a transformed wilderness. It is a blindingly white
landscape where the everyday shrubs and boulders
have become strange, hump-backed forms of
fantastic creatures in a snow sculptor's garden.

Coyote is the first out, the
first witness to the wonder. He
licks up a mouthful of snow, then runs
headlong in delight across the clearing,
plowing the drifts with his muzzle.

Snowshoe Hare is an early riser, too. He stands near a hickory stump and nibbles at sprigs of laurel. His white fur renders him all but invisible. A good thing, for Hare knows Coyote is awake and about.

Beneath the cold blanket,
White-Footed Mouse scratches out a
tunnel along the ground, snatching up nuts and
seeds like tiny treasures to be carried to her burrow.

A thin layer of ice gleams at the edges of John's Brook
as wild turkeys glide through the open air and
roost side by side, gobbling in strange conversation.

Upper limbs of the woodlands,
shaken bare, reach like outstretched
arms and splayed fingers into a sky as blue as a sea.
Fronds of sumac and twisted vines of virginia creeper
fringe the forest's edge, decorated in berries of red and blue.

Blue jays crowd a stand of balsam and hop from
branch to branch, sending down lumps of snow
in soft plops. Their shrill chatter fills the woods
as if to announce the first snowfall.

Otter and his family are out, too. It is a time for play. They line up atop a steep riverbank. Father goes first. He belly-flops over the edge and onto the slope. In mid-slide, he rolls onto his back and splashes upside down into the water. His family sits back on their haunches and barks their approval. One after another, they glide, roll, and wriggle down the slick ramp and plunge into the icy water.

Red Fox is last to rise. He bursts
through the drift that blocks his den,
dressed for the occasion in his splendid
scarlet coat. For just a moment, he
soaks in the warm sunshine. But even
he must celebrate by scampering in
dizzy circles and snapping at the
ground in a silly game of
catch-my-shadow.

Overhead in a flying vee,
Canada geese beat their wings and honk.

Winter Wren cheers from a treetop below.

Wherever one looks there is
jubilation for the once-a-year arrival.

Everywhere, everywhere,
there is celebration for the coming
of the Adirondack Winter.